FLY HIGH, FLY GUY!

Tedd Arnold

Cartwheel
·B·O·O·K·S· ®

SCHOLASTIC INC.
New York   Toronto   London   Auckland
Sydney   Mexico City   New Delhi   Hong Kong

For Christene
—T.A.

ISBN-13: 978-0-545-21125-3
ISBN-10: 0-545-21125-5

Copyright © 2008 by Tedd Arnold.
Published by Scholastic Inc. SCHOLASTIC, CARTWHEEL BOOKS, and
associated logos are trademarks and/or registered trademarks of Scholastic Inc.

26   16 17 18 19/0

Printed in the U.S.A.   40

First Scholastic paperback printing, September 2009

A boy had a pet fly.
He named him Fly Guy.
Fly Guy could say
the boy's name—

Chapter 1

One day Buzz said,
"It's time to take
a road trip."

Fly Guy wanted to go, too.
"He's too little," said Mom.
"He might get lost."

"Sorry," said Dad.
"Fly Guy stays home."

He shut the trunk.
"Okay, let's hit the road!"

The family drove and drove.

They stopped for a picnic.
Mom opened the trunk.
Fly Guy flew out.

Dad said, "How did
he get in there?"

"Just don't lose him,"
said Mom and Dad.
"Now, let's eat!"

Chapter 2

They drove to the beach.

Then it was time to go.
Mom and Dad said,
"Is Fly Guy lost?"

"No," said Buzz.
"Here he is!"

They drove to
the art museum.

KISS

Then it was time to go.
Mom and Dad said,
"Is Fly Guy lost?"

"No," said Buzz.
"Here he is!"

They drove to
the fun park.

Then it was time to go.
Mom and Dad said,
"Is Fly Guy lost?"

"No," said Buzz.

"Here he is!"

Chapter 3

"It's time to go home,"
said Mom.
"Let's hit the road,"
said Dad.

They drove

and drove

and drove

and drove

and drove

and drove

and drove

and drove

and drove

and drove

and drove

and drove

and drove

But they did not get home.
"We're lost," said Mom
and Dad.

Buzz and Fly Guy had an idea.
Buzz said, "Fly high, Fly Guy!"

Fly Guy flew high into the sky.
He used his super fly eyes
to spy their house.

Fly Guy led the way home.

"Thank you, Fly Guy,"
said Mom and Dad.
"You saved the day!
Yay, Fly Guy!"